Peer Pressure

The ball was against the back wall. Eric squeezed his way underneath the bleachers trying to reach it. The second his fingers touched the ball . . .

. . . the lights went out.

BAM! At the far end of the gym, the first set of bleachers suddenly slammed back.

"Hey! What gives?"

BAM! The second set of bleachers accordioned back to the wall, with an earsplitting noise. Then . . . *BAM!* The third set of bleachers flew back with such force that its wood splintered in all directions.

Eric was behind the fifth set of bleachers. He would have to climb through a maze of iron to get out.

"*HEEELLLLP!*" he screamed. "*Somebody stop it! Help me!*" He began to run, trying to squeeze between the bars. Then he heard the grinding of gears as the bleachers around him started to move . . .

have read

Bad Sign

A novelization by Easton Royce
Based on the television series

THE (X) FILES™

created by Chris Carter
Based on the teleplay
written by Chris Carter

HarperTrophy®
A Division of HarperCollins*Publishers*

Chapter One

Beneath the billion pinprick stars shining in the clear night sky, beneath the eight unblinking eyes of the other planets, beneath the cold disk of the full moon, a solemn ritual was taking place. A dozen cars and pickup trucks were parked in a circle. In the center stood a group of teenagers, the tears in their eyes lit only by the stars, the moon, and the candles they held in their hands.

Jay "Boom" DeBoom zipped up his letterman's jacket with his free hand and brought the candle a little closer to his face. He didn't want to see the eyes of those around him. They were all looking at him, because Boom was supposed to give the eulogy. The one they gave at the real funeral didn't seem right. It wasn't the kind of eulogy Bruno would have wanted. So his friends had gathered out here to pay their own last respects.

"I remember me and him all the way back to kindergarten." Boom finally said, his words breathing steam into the cold night. "He was, I don't know, like a brother or something."

Boom turned to look at the little shrine they had set up. A collection of Bruno's things—his senior class picture, his football helmet, a couple of trophies—sat on a nearby tree stump.

"Bruno and me, we had some good times that I'll never forget . . . and junk like that." Now Boom moved the candle away from his face just a bit, so the others couldn't see his eyes getting moist. He had sworn he wouldn't cry, and the fact that he was on the verge of doing it made him mad. Mad at Bruno's killers, and at all of the things that were going on around them—things that were beyond their control. He looked up at the others.

"Now we have to stick together and protect each other, because that's what Bruno would have wanted. And 'cause they say the cult will try and get more of us. We can't let that happen."

Boom glanced down at Bruno's picture again, his image pale blue in the moonlight. "So we gotta kick some butt . . . like I'm sure Bruno's doing in heaven right now."

He barely got the words out before his eyes filled with tears. He blew out his candle, and a thin line of smoke drifted up from the cinder of the wick toward the cold sky. He left the circle quickly, fighting to get his emotions under control. Bruno's death hurt more than anything he could remember—more than when that other kid had died. He had barely known that guy, but Bruno had always been his closest friend. Who would have thought that an evil cult could rise up in a friendly town like Comity? How could it have happened? He leaned his head against his pickup and smashed his fist against its hard body, hoping the pain in his knuckles would drive away the pain of Bruno's death.

The light around him changed slightly, and he turned. Two girls were heading toward him timidly, cupping their candles against the wind. Boom blinked, clearing the tears that clouded his eyes. It was Terri Roberts and Margi Kleinjan—two cheerleaders who always went around together like they were connected at the hip. They'd both had crushes on Bruno, Boom remembered.

"Are you okay, Boom?" Terri asked.

"Yeah," said Boom, still too choked up to say anything else. He kept his face turned from them, wiping the tears from his eyes. Margi took a step closer.

"What you said back there—that was beautiful, Boom."

"Yeah," Boom said, taking a quick glance at them. In the candlelight he could see that the mascara around their eyes hadn't run at all. No tears. *It hits everybody differently*, he thought. A lot of people were still in shock.

"Did you hear who the cult is supposed to be coming after next?" Terri asked. Boom shook his head.

"A blond virgin," Margi said, with a sickened expression. Boom took in the worried looks on their faces. He suddenly realized it was time for him to be strong, for their sake and for everyone else's. With Bruno gone, he was Big Man on Campus. The guy everyone looked up to.

"Come on. I'll give you two a ride home," he told the girls, and tossed his dead candle into the bed of his pickup. It clattered over the cans and sports gear that cluttered his truck bed, coming to rest on a coil of rope. That rope had been used in a game of tug-of-war at the homecoming picnic. Bruno had been the anchor on their team. Boom stared at the rope for a moment, idly wondering how they'd ever keep from being dragged into the mud now without Bruno behind them.

Strange winds crosscut the fog into dense pockets along the deserted country road. Boom tried to keep his attention on his driving. On the radio, some sad song played. *Too sad*, thought Boom, and he turned it off.

Beside him, Terri and Margi were talking

about that blond-virgin thing again. It made Boom a bit uncomfortable to hear girls talk about that kind of stuff right in front of him.

"Our moms are always saying, 'Wait until you're married. Don't just give it away,'" Terri said.

"And then some cult member wants to kidnap you," said Margi, "and sacrifice you, because you *are* a virgin." They turned to Boom for a response, but he gave them none.

"How do they know you're a virgin, anyway?" asked Margi.

Terri shook her head. "I don't even want to *think* about *that*!" And then they both turned to Boom.

"You're not a virgin, are you, Boom?" asked Margi.

"Uh . . . no," said Boom, not sure if he sounded convincing enough. "And I'm not blond, either. So I guess I'm safe." He offered up a nervous laugh.

"You know," Terri said, "maybe if we *weren't* virgins, we wouldn't be so scared."

"Yeah," echoed Margi.

6

Boom took his eyes off the road to take a quick look at them. The girls were dead serious.

Well, he thought, *here's something you don't see every day.*

This sort of thing wasn't really his style. But giving up their virginity was in their own best interest, wasn't it? He might just be saving their lives.

There was a dirt road up ahead, and Boom made a quick decision to turn down it. His tires squealed as they left the pavement.

"Thanks, Boom," said Margi, gently grasping his arm. He could feel her long pink-painted nails digging into his biceps, even through his Grover Cleveland Gruffs jacket.

Terri glanced at them and looked disgusted. "Don't thank him *yet*, Margi," Terri said coldly. "And anyway, it was my idea."

Margi scowled at Terri. "Well, *I* was the one who liked Boom first!"

"Was not!" said Terri.

"Was too!" said Margi.

Boom sighed. Everyone knew that when these two fought, it was tooth and nail—and

God help anyone who got caught in the middle. He floored the accelerator as they headed up into steep terrain. "Girls, let's just get it over with, okay?"

They both turned on him then, their eyes as cold as an ice storm. Terri released her grip on his arm. "Just what do you mean by that?" she asked nastily.

Boom quickly shut his mouth, suddenly wishing that he had just stayed on the road and taken the girls straight home. With the looks they were giving him now, he suspected that this little scrimmage wasn't going to be any fun at all.

The eye of Venus still pierced the dawn sky as two squad cars sped down the dirt road that led into the woods. The police figured that Jay DeBoom had just pulled an all-nighter with his friends, to talk about that other kid's death. But DeBoom's mother insisted that Jay would never do that. The fresh skid marks turning off the highway and onto the dirt road gave them a clear path to follow. They figured they'd find the kid asleep in his pickup, but that wasn't the case. His pickup was there, but no one was inside. Its doors wide open, the truck sat at the end of the road before the face of a granite cliff.

"Over here!" shouted one of the deputies. As they climbed a pile of boulders to get a better look, the situation suddenly became very clear.

A pair of feet dangled a few inches above their heads. As they turned their eyes up, they could see a varsity jacket with the name DEBOOM across the back . . .

. . . and a rope around the dead kid's neck.

His body swung slightly with the wind, dangling from a long rope tied somewhere above the high cliff before them.

"Oh God, is he dead?" asked one deputy, as if there were any question.

"Yeah. Looks like he hung himself," said another.

As they left to radio the coroner, they thought they heard the tinkle of far-off laughter. But it must have been a trick of the wind.

Chapter Two

Scully's mood sank with every passing mile.

She glanced over at Mulder, who was behind the wheel of their rented car. He seemed lost in his own thoughts, staring through the windshield at the highway ahead of them. It had, in fact, been nearly an hour since either of them had spoken a word to the other.

Maybe her silence was due in part to her initial lack of interest in the case. When Mulder had first approached her with it, she hadn't exactly been overjoyed.

The residents of the town of Comity believed that a satanic cult was preying on them.

"Mulder, do you have any idea how unlikely that is?" she had said to him back in their office. The fact was, the FBI had investigated dozens of similar cases and had proved, to her satisfaction at least, that no such activity was going on. In almost every case, panic and hysteria alone were the only evils responsible.

Mulder, as usual, disagreed. "This case is different," he had insisted. "I looked up those other cases. In most of them, there was no evidence of any crime at all, let alone a murder. This time there are three bodies."

"A drowning, the victim of a car accident, and a suicide," Scully had replied, referring to the file Mulder had handed her. "Hardly proof of devil worship."

But Mulder wouldn't listen.

Well, Scully thought, *it certainly isn't the first time.* In fact, it was their frequent opposition that made them so good at what they did.

No matter how initially skeptical Scully was of Mulder's sometimes bizarre theories—that aliens were responsible for a disappearance, or that an ancient curse was behind a string of remarkable accidents—she approached their cases with a sense of adventure. Sometimes with a feeling nearing exhilaration.

But not this time.

The closer they got to Comity, the more Scully wished for this case to be over already. They were wasting their time. There were so many more-important things that they could be doing. She wondered if Mulder felt the same way.

She looked over at him, waiting for him to acknowledge her, but his eyes didn't even flicker in her direction.

Without a word Mulder pulled off the highway and onto a narrow country road. They drove for a few more miles in silence, past woods and open fields. Finally they came to a lonely stop sign at an even more lonely intersection.

While Mulder fumbled for the directions that had been faxed to them by the Comity Police Department, Scully checked the map.

"Turn right," she instructed.

Mulder checked the barely legible directions and shook his head.

"It says here to turn left."

Scully looked at her map, trying to understand why. "At the intersection?"

"At the stoplight," Mulder said. His even tone, Scully noticed, betrayed the smallest hint of impatience. That wasn't like him.

She looked from her partner to the red octagonal sign outside their window.

"This isn't a stoplight," she said. "It's a stop sign."

"I'm sure the detective who wrote this *meant* stop *sign*," Mulder insisted. This time the irritation in his voice wasn't even concealed.

Scully shook her head. "I'd turn right."

Mulder stepped on the gas and turned left.

After a few miles it was clear they had gone the wrong way.

Without looking at Scully, Mulder swung the car in a lazy U and headed back. Scully resisted the urge to say "I told you so."

A few miles past the intersection where Mulder had made the wrong turn, Scully realized it was a good thing she had resisted . . . because she too was wrong. Mulder turned the car around again and they were back where they'd started.

"Maybe we should have just gone straight," Mulder proposed. It was more a question than a statement.

"Is that your professional opinion?" Scully chided.

Soon they came to another intersection. This one was regulated by a stoplight.

Scully pointed out the windshield. "Stoplight," she said. She pointed back the way they had come. "Stop sign."

"Stop *it*," Mulder said. "I got the point." He turned the car to the left, and they proceeded without further incident to the Comity Police Department.

At the police station they displayed their IDs to the heavyset desk sergeant. Mulder told him they were there to see Detective White. The sergeant shook his head—then winced and put his hand up to his forehead.

"Are you all right?" Scully asked, concerned.

The man nodded very slowly.

"It's just a headache. Had it for a couple weeks," he said. "It won't go away, no matter

14

what I take." He took a deep breath and exhaled slowly. Then he said, "Detective White is attending the funeral of Jay DeBoom, the latest victim of the . . ."

The man hesitated, and searched the faces of the two agents as if he wasn't sure he could trust them with the horrible truth.

Mulder got the directions to the funeral home, and they returned to their car.

As they drove through the town, Mulder took a look around, trying to form an impression of the community they would spend the next few days investigating.

Mulder stopped at a light. Two men sitting in the car next to him were screaming at each other. This wouldn't have struck him as strange, except that the car was a police cruiser and the two men were uniformed officers. When the two policemen noticed Mulder and Scully staring, they stopped arguing, hit their siren, and sped away through the red light.

The light turned green and Mulder drove

on. On the next block he saw a man in a business suit sitting at the curb, crying his eyes out. Then, at the corner of the block, he saw a liquor store with a line out the door.

"Is there a big lottery drawing tonight?" Mulder asked, pointing to the line.

"Not that I know of," Scully answered.

"So all those people buying booze—"

Mulder quickly slammed on the brakes. A well-dressed elderly woman had just darted across the street in front of the car.

"Hey!" Mulder yelled at her through the window. He was going to add "Be careful," but the woman glared back at him with such intensity that the words died in his throat.

They were the angriest eyes he had ever seen. They had locked on him with such utter hatred that he didn't even notice that the old woman had given him the finger before turning and darting away.

"I have to tell you, Scully," Mulder said to his partner as he carefully accelerated. "If satanists aren't preying on this town . . . something is."

Chapter Three

When Scully and Mulder entered the funeral home, the service was nearly over. The closed coffin at the front of the room was draped with flowers, and the dead teen's senior portrait stood on the lid in a gilt frame. The minister was just inviting friends and family members to come up and share their personal remembrances of the deceased. Only a few took the opportunity.

Mulder and Scully, standing in the back, gazed around the packed chapel. Most of the adults were in the first few rows. The two sobbing in the very front were probably the boy's parents. The rest of the pews were filled with high-school-age kids. Many of the young men were wearing letterman jackets. The kid must have been popular.

An attractive blond woman approached the two agents.

"Agent Mulder?" she asked softly. Mulder nodded, surprised that she knew his name. She put out a hand. "I'm Detective White."

Mulder took her hand and held it. This was their local police contact?

From her fashionable business attire, he might have taken her for a junior executive with an investment bank. From her silky blond hair and pert, upturned nose, he could have taken her for a former model. But—

"I never would have taken you for a detective," he said suavely, even bowing slightly.

Scully felt like she was going to gag. *Not a pretty young thing like you*, she thought resentfully, wondering if Mulder was actually going to kiss the woman's hand.

But he simply shook it. Detective White turned to Scully.

Scully shook her hand. "Agent Dana Scully." Then she added, with an acid smile, "*Miss* White."

"*Detective* White," the policewoman emphasized.

Scully instantly hated her. She didn't know why, but she did.

Detective White nodded toward the coffin at the front of the hall. "His friends called him Boom," she said softly. "He was the quarterback of the football team. Well liked. A leader." She shook her head. "He was looking forward to college—until they found him hanged in the woods two days ago. The third death of a high-school boy in as many weeks."

Mulder moved forward, close to her, and whispered, "In your fax you said there were strong suspicions of a satanic cult at work."

White nodded. "It's the popular opinion around here. Wildly popular, actually."

Scully wasn't sure if she was being intentionally excluded from the conversation, but she didn't like it. "Based on what evidence?" she interjected.

White turned to her. "Various eyewitness accounts of strange rituals being conducted."

"And do you have physical evidence of these rituals?" Scully asked.

"No. Just the victims."

Scully sighed. Just as she thought. "So . . . you have nothing concrete to connect these deaths to cult practices?" she asked wearily.

Mulder leaned over until his face was between Scully's and Detective White's. He smiled at the policewoman reassuringly. "If you detect a hint of skepticism in Agent Scully's voice," he whispered, "it's only because the FBI has collected overwhelming evidence that most claims of ritual abuse by satanic cults have no merit whatsoever."

Scully looked at Mulder, confused. His words seemed to be backing her up, but his tone betrayed an underlying edge of sarcasm.

"Is that true?" Detective White asked, surprised.

"Don't ask me," he shrugged, and jerked his thumb at Scully.

Scully took a breath and recited the FBI's conclusions, based on the bureau's prior investigations into similar accusations of cult activity. "All of the accounts we studied have turned out to be false or imagined. A series of deaths occurred, and these tragic, but *random*, events were linked to cults only as a result of hysteria, denial, or misplaced blame. In every case we studied, the cult turned out to be imaginary."

Detective White didn't back down. "What about the cases you didn't study?" she asked. Then she let her gaze wander around the funeral chapel. "You'll have a hard time convincing the locals that this is just a case of 'hysteria.'" Her eyes stopped on two girls sitting in the next-to-last row.

"Especially," White continued, "after hearing the stories of the two girls who were there the night Boom died."

She gestured toward them. Mulder and Scully looked at the two pretty sixteen-year-old girls. One had dark blond hair and the other's was light blond, but their faces were similar and their dresses nearly identical.

"Terri Roberts and Margi Kleinjan," said Detective White. "They're really distraught over this, the poor things."

"Who interviewed them?" Scully asked.

"I did," replied White.

Scully sized up Detective White. The woman was young, Scully thought, and the town was small, but would she make the most obvious mistake? Only one way to find out.

"Together or separately?" Scully asked, hoping to hear her answer, "Separately."

"Together," said Detective White. "Why?"

Scully sighed. "Well, now you have no way of knowing if they made the story up, do you?"

Detective White shook her head adamantly. "No. These are good kids we're talking about. Outstanding students. And the details they gave—I doubt they could have made them up."

Scully became decidedly smug. "Let me guess," she said, cocking her head to the side. "They told you about a wild beast appearing at a Black Mass, people dressed in dark robes—

oh, and there's always a reference to a snake in there somewhere . . ."

Mulder watched Detective White's face. It registered increasing levels of shock as Scully went down her list, item after item apparently matching the testimony White had heard from the two girls.

Scully continued her litany: ". . . um, the sacrifice on a stone altar of an infant—one that, oddly enough, no one ever reported missing." She looked at Detective White sweetly. "Or the sacrifice of a blond virgin."

Detective White was speechless for a moment, searching for the words to answer Scully. "Yes," she said, nodding.

Loud but muffled voices were raised near the front of the room. Detective White glanced in that direction, then back at Scully and Mulder. They couldn't see who was making the commotion.

"Excuse me," Detective White said, and quickly walked down the center aisle toward the casket.

"Where is she going?" Scully asked.

Mulder watched her go. "You don't suppose she's a virgin?"

Scully snorted. "I doubt she's even a real blond."

At the front of the chapel, Detective White moved toward a side door, past the front row. The raised voices were coming from behind the closed door.

Now Scully could make out two distinct voices. A deep voice was insisting, "Sir, you can't go in there—" while simultaneously the other voice, a frantic whine, was pleading, "Let me through."

Detective White opened the door. But she was pushed back into the chapel by the onrushing force of a wild-eyed man in a blue windbreaker.

His sandy hair was mussed, his mustache needed grooming, and his unbuttoned shirt was askew, but the wildest thing about him was his eyes. Even from the back of the room, Scully could see in them the sparks of an internal short-circuit.

The man was clearly caught up in a frenzy.

He darted past Detective White and took a position directly in front of the grieving parents. Then he cried out, "How long are we going to stand by and watch our children die? While this unspeakable evil runs free in our town?"

Detective White moved to the man and stood in front of him. "Bob, this is not the time—"

"Not the time?" he cried in amazement. "*Not the time?* What are you waiting for? A sign in the sky?"

His words were finding a receptive audience. Several of the mourners shouted words of agreement. Scully looked at Mulder and cocked her head toward the crowd. This was what she was talking about, the contagious power of mass hysteria—virulent and overpowering.

Detective White put a gentle hand on the man's shoulder and spoke soothingly to him, but he pulled away.

"Let go of me!" he shouted, then ran up the steps to the chapel's pulpit. He stopped behind the flower-bedecked coffin and exhorted the crowd like a revivalist preacher. "My kids say they can feel Satan's presence in the town! I can too—can't *you*? Can't you feel it? We've got to take action! Somehow we've got to drive him out of our community!"

Detective White walked up the steps toward the frightened and angry man, but she was fighting a rising tide of sentiment in the room that agreed with him.

While Scully watched Detective White's performance, Mulder tried to get a clear sense of the mood of the crowd. He noticed that the two teenage girls Detective White had pointed out earlier were now holding hands and looking intensely toward the front of the room. Mulder could see that the man's accusations were affecting them.

Around the girls, the other mourners' expressions suddenly changed from righteous anger to fear and surprise. The room quickly grew quiet, as even the wild man in the windbreaker fell silent. Mulder looked to the front of the room.

Small wisps of smoke now rose from the dead boy's coffin, seeping from the seam of the lid.

People began to whisper urgently to each other, pointing out the smoke to those who had not yet noticed it. Then pointing became unnecessary, as the wisps became billows of smoke pouring from the coffin.

The whispers turned to cries of alarm.

"Don't panic," Detective White shouted, panicking herself. "Everyone, please, stay calm." Standing behind the coffin, she was barely visible through the curtain of smoke.

People screamed when the glass in the frame of Boom's picture shattered, and the coffin burst into flames. Suddenly everyone was running, knocking over chairs as they thundered from the hall. One young man was bowled over by the crush. Mulder leaped forward to help him up before he was trampled underfoot.

"People, please!" Detective White shouted from the front of the room. But it was too late. Her voice was barely audible over the pande-monium.

The flowers on the coffin were quickly consumed by the licking flames. Smoke filled the chapel, but the fire, so far, was confined to the coffin.

Mulder nodded to Scully, and gestured toward the fire and smoke. "Maybe we're just 'imagining' that, too," he said dryly, before heading to the lobby to look for a fire extinguisher.

Scully glared at her partner as she pulled her cell phone out of her pocket to call the fire department.

Neither of them noticed the two girls, Terri and Margi, still sitting in their seats. They were the only two mourners in the chapel who hadn't panicked when the fire began. They were staring at the burning casket—as if transfixed by the scene—with an intensity that transcended this particular place and this particular time.

Chapter Four

In a small interrogation room that caught only hints of daylight through drawn venetian blinds, Scully sat across a cold metal table from Terri Roberts. Scully already knew she wouldn't buy the girl's story. She hadn't bought anything she had heard from the moment she and Mulder had arrived in this town. It was as if there was something about this place, something that made her clothes feel itchy and her hair stand on end when anyone spoke to her—even Mulder and his incessantly calm voice was an irritation.

"My name is Terri Roberts," the girl began. "I go to Grover Cleveland Alexander High School. I'm a senior with a 3.98 grade point average."

Scully pushed the microphone closer to the girl. Young Terri Roberts seemed so vulnerable now—sweet and innocent. Watching her, Scully told herself she should give the girl the benefit of the doubt, and listen carefully to anything she said.

"I'm on the cheerleading yell squad with my best friend, Margi," Terri continued. "We plan to go to college together in the fall."

"Can you tell me exactly what happened the night of Jay DeBoom's death?" Scully asked.

Terri looked down, took a deep breath, and began. "Boom—Jay, that is—was just giving us a ride home in his truck, when all of a sudden he swerved off the road—like he was possessed or something. At first we thought he knew a shortcut. I mean, we trusted Boom. But then he seemed to get very serious. He stopped talking to us and just floored the accelerator down that dirt road. That's when we started to get a little bit worried. He stopped his truck once we were deep into the woods. Then he turned off the headlights and

I could see a light up ahead, like some people were there. He pushed us out of the car and forced us to walk into a clearing, where about twenty people in black robes stood in a circle, holding black candles. I tried to see their faces under their hoods, but those hoods were so big, I couldn't recognize anyone. I knew they were up to no good."

Scully tried to lock her eyeballs into place, to prevent them from rolling.

"How did you know they were up to no good?" she asked . . .

". . . And how did you know they were up to no good?" asked Mulder in the next interrogation room, which was separated from Scully and Terri by nine inches of cinder block and soundproofing. Mulder had a hunch that the two girls' stories would be remarkably similar. But what he didn't know, at that moment, was that they were identical. Word for word, breath for breath. If they had been videotaped, their hand gestures and body language would have mirrored each other perfectly.

"They were standing around this altar," said Margi Kleinjan. "A big, black, shiny stone. And one of them had a long knife with a snake head on the end of the handle with bright red eyes—they were rubies, I think. Off in the bushes was some sort of animal. It was huge and growling—but I couldn't tell what it was . . . and I thought for sure we were dead, because we heard they were going to sacrifice a blond virgin. Boom pushed us toward them, and they grabbed us, holding our hands behind our backs. But it turned out they weren't going to sacrifice us just yet. Instead, they brought out a little baby. They unwrapped it from its blanket, and . . . and . . ."

Margi's chin started quivering and she put her hand up to her eyes. Her voice became squeaky as she spoke. ". . . And the man with the knife started to say something. A prayer, I guess. He was saying something about sacrificing the baby because it wasn't christened yet, and how they were going to bury it in a mass grave on the outskirts of town, with all the other babies they'd killed. And then the whole group started chanting, and the man with the knife raised the blade up over the baby . . . and that's when Terri and I broke free and ran for our lives. I don't know what happened next, because I didn't look back. I guess maybe they killed Boom after that—because they blamed him for letting us get away. Or maybe he just killed himself when he realized what an awful, awful thing it was that he had gotten involved in." Margi broke down crying after that, her hair dangling down, making hissing noises on the tape as it brushed over the microphone.

Mulder looked at Margi closely to see if her tears were real. Yes, they seemed to be. If this girl wasn't telling the truth, she was putting on a very convincing show.

Chapter Five

Detective White reached down and turned off the tape recorder, cutting off the echoes of Margi's final, wracking sobs. She looked from Mulder to Scully and back again.

The silence stretched on as each of them sorted through their own reactions to what they had just heard.

Detective White finally spoke, her emotions evident in her voice. "You see?" she said. "The stories are virtually identical. One corroborates the other."

"Or it shows that they concocted it together," Scully pointed out evenly. Then, a little more heatedly: "Look, I don't suppose there have been any actual reports of stolen infants—let alone any mass graves uncovered anywhere in town?"

Detective White shook her head.

"Have you found a bloodstained altar," Scully went on, "or any other evidence of this cult's activity?"

"No," the policewoman said. "We haven't—yet."

Scully shook her head with finality. "You won't—ever. The details in these accounts could have been taken from any magazine or newspaper. As horrific as they sound, the stories these girls told are just bad clichés."

Mulder had been leaning against the wall near Scully. Now he stood and walked around the table, until he was on the other side, standing next to Detective White. He leaned closer to her, grinning.

"If you detect a hint of impatience in Agent Scully's voice," he said, "it's because the FBI's study found that, in most of these cases, the witnesses' statements were prompted by the rumors and stories already circulating in the town. The testimony, in turn, fed more rumors, when there was, in fact, nothing to support any of it."

Once again, Scully noticed, his words seemed to agree with her position, but his arch tone seemed to argue against it. Or was she just imagining that?

Detective White looked at the two agents. This time it was her turn to sound impatient. "Then how do you explain the coffin at the funeral bursting into flames?"

Mulder leaned even closer to her and said, confidentially, "Don't ask me." Then, pointing at Scully, he added, "But I'm sure Agent Scully has an explanation."

Scully stared at Mulder, but he refused to meet her gaze. Finally she said, in a definitive tone, "Yes, in fact, I do."

Detective White led the way to the police morgue.

In the middle of the room, they saw the charred coffin resting on a wide steel table. A plastic sheet, dotted with police evidence stickers, was draped over the casket.

Scully threw back the sheet and heaved open the lid without hesitation. A few gray flakes of ash spun into the air as the lid went up. Scully peered down at the remains.

Much of Jay DeBoom's burial suit, and most of his shirt, had been burned away by the fire. So had a large portion of the casket's lining.

Where the dead teen's skin was visible, a few areas had been charred black.

"There *have* been incidents where the embalming fluids used to preserve the body have caused chemical reactions, in a few cases causing fires to break out," Scully explained.

She looked a little closer and nodded. "I see nothing here that would suggest otherwise."

Mulder and Detective White were looking over her shoulder.

"What's that?" asked Detective White, pointing at the boy's chest.

"What's *what*?" asked Scully a little testily.

"That pattern, there on his chest," White answered, moving her finger a little closer to one of the blackened patches on the boy's skin.

"Pattern?" asked Scully.

"Yeah," Mulder confirmed. "I see it."

Scully looked closer at the burned area they were referring to. All she saw was an irregular shape, blistered and blackened, a vaguely triangular area with two narrower triangles protruding from the base.

"What do you see?" Scully asked.

"It looks like a goat," Mulder answered slowly. "Or maybe a horned beast."

Scully looked at him. "A horned beast?"

"Yeah," Mulder insisted, indicating the area again, more precisely this time. "Right here."

Scully shook her head. "I think you're both seeing something that isn't there."

"Right here," said Detective White, apparently under the impression that Scully still didn't know where to look. She jabbed her finger at the two narrow triangles. "See? You have to see those horns right there."

"No, I *don't* see horns right there," Scully said. She spoke with such frosty finality that Detective White withdrew her hand and looked over at Mulder, puzzled. He shrugged apologetically.

"I assume you'll call me if you need anything else," Detective White said to the back of Scully's head. Then she smiled politely at Mulder and left the room.

Scully was preparing to examine the boy's body more closely. She pulled a latex glove over one hand, releasing the material with a loud snap once it felt snug.

Mulder's eyes followed Detective White out of the room. The snap of the latex brought his attention back to Scully. His irritation level with her peaked. What had gotten into his partner? he wondered. Why in the world would she offend their police contact like that? Where was that going to get them? They needed the cooperation of the local police in order to operate efficiently.

And why wouldn't she admit that the burn mark on the boy's chest bore an uncanny resemblance to a horned beast—a potent symbol as ancient as time?

He leaned over to speak to Scully, who was

herself leaning over the casket. With patience stretched to the breaking point, he forced himself to speak evenly.

"If it's no bother . . ." he began. "If it's not too big a deal . . . if you *don't mind* . . . maybe you could get me a few photographs of that thing which bears absolutely no resemblance to a horned beast."

It took a lot of effort, at this point, to speak to her with such restraint. As he turned and left the morgue, he hoped she appreciated it.

Apparently she didn't.

"Sure," she said, pulling a matching latex glove onto her other hand and snapping it loud enough for him to hear from the hallway. "Fine. Whatever."

Chapter Six

Irritated by his partner's behavior, Mulder walked through town as the sun began to set.

Why was Scully acting so annoying lately? Was she being especially offensive? After all this time they had worked together, was her obtuse skepticism finally getting to him?

No, he decided. That didn't ring true. He always appreciated her point of view—they balanced each other perfectly. At times, he pushed her further than she would willingly go, but she kept him grounded.

And besides, he grinned to himself, he always knew he was really on to something when he could convince *her*. She was a valuable asset—he couldn't have gotten through many cases without her.

So why was this case different? . . . Why were *they* different?

He pondered as he walked.

He wasn't conscious of where he was going, but somehow he wasn't surprised when he looked up at where he finally had stopped. He was outside Detective White's house.

Angela White.

He wasn't sure what he was feeling about her, or why. He really didn't want to analyze it too deeply. Oh, certainly there was an attraction there. But she was an integral part of this case, and Mulder was, after all, a professional.

He was turning to go when he saw a streak of gold dart under the rattan chair on her porch. Mulder took a few steps closer for a better look.

Two bright yellow dots stared out at him from the darkness under the chair. Mulder stayed very still. After a few moments a gold tabby emerged from beneath the chair.

Mulder crouched down and put his hand out, and the cat slowly, gingerly, approached.

It sniffed, and then licked his outstretched fingers. The little sandpaper tongue against his fingertips made Mulder smile, and he cradled the cat in his hands as he stood up.

He checked the tag on its collar. Sure enough, underneath the cat's name, *Tabitha*, in smaller letters he read, ANGELA WHITE.

He rang the doorbell and waited patiently until Angela opened the door.

Detective White, he reminded himself. It was a difficult thing to remember when he looked at her, dressed so casually, and looking so gorgeous, in a tight red sweater and black slacks, her hair loose and falling freely to her shoulders.

He looked at her, and all he could say was "Hi."

"Hi," she answered, crossing her arms and leaning against the doorjamb, keeping Mulder at bay on the porch. "What are you doing with my cat?"

He looked down dumbly at the cat in his hands, as though he wasn't sure how it had gotten there. "Oh. I thought, with the threat of satanic animal sacrifice looming, maybe you should keep her inside."

Mulder handed the cat to her. Angela gently put her pet on the floor behind her, inside the house. Then she turned her attention back to Mulder.

"I thought the FBI's research would have debunked that theory," she said coolly.

Mulder sighed. "First off, I'd like to apologize for my partner's rudeness. She tends to be a bit skeptical—"

Angela chuckled at the understatement, and Mulder rushed to continue the thought.

"But usually skeptical in a wonderful way . . . nothing like she was today. . ." Mulder trailed off. He was sounding like an idiot, and he knew it. He took a breath and tried again. "Personally . . . I try to keep a more open mind."

Angela nodded and smiled. "So," she said, "that still doesn't explain what you're doing at my house."

Mulder shot her a sly look. "I was hoping you could help me solve the mystery of the horny beast."

x x x

Less than an hour later, Mulder and Detective White stood before a small building on a dark road near the edge of town. It was a place people rarely visited, or at least rarely admitted to visiting. Mulder looked up at the sign in front of him. Neon letters within a zodiac circle spelled out ZIRINKA: ASTROLOGY, NUMEROLOGY, RUNES, AND READINGS.

With the stars as bright as they are tonight, thought Mulder as he and Detective White stepped up to the porch, *you could almost believe in celestial powers. If the moon can drag entire oceans, creating tides, why can't the stars and planets and moon affect* living *things as well?* He grinned, wondering what Scully would think of this decidedly unscientific theory. Detective White took the grin to mean something else.

"I know this seems silly," she said, "but if anyone can identify an occult symbol, it's Zirinka."

Zirinka, however, was not pleased to see them after working hours. But she did consent to look at the picture they had brought. It was a blowup of Jay DeBoom's charred chest.

"It's those horns we're worried about," prompted Mulder.

Zirinka was a gutsy woman who seemed more like a New York cop than a small-town fortune teller. She studied the picture and then looked up at Mulder and Detective White. "Let me get this straight. You say you see *horns* here?"

Mulder thought if there were one person in this town he could count on *not* to be skeptical, it would be someone like Zirinka. But apparently even fortune tellers drew the line somewhere. "You don't see what looks like a beast, or maybe a goat, there?"

She raised an eyebrow and grinned. "This is a trick, right? You're trying to entrap me, aren't you?"

Detective White took a step closer. "No one's trying to entrap you, Zirinka."

Zirinka tossed the picture back to Mulder, and stood.

"Oh yeah? There's a lot of loonies running around this town. Some of them would like to think I'm part of this 'cult' everyone's talking about. But I'm just a number cruncher, trying to make an honest living here."

"Accountant of the stars," offered Mulder.

"Exactly," said Zirinka. "Planets move, I tell people where they are, and what it's supposed to mean."

"What do *you* think is going on, if I may ask?" Mulder inquired.

Zirinka gave it to him straight. "I think this town has lost its marbles," she said. "You'd think I would have seen it coming, but it's hard, being a small-business owner." She glanced at a desk so messy it was impossible to see the color of the wood underneath the papers. "See all this paperwork?" she said. "If I'd known astrology meant pushing paper, I would have been a dental hygienist."

"You said you should have seen it coming. What did you mean by that?" Mulder asked.

Zirinka looked at him like it was obvious. "We're heading into a rare planetary alignment," she told them. "A *syzygy*—three celestial bodies in perfect alignment. And these particular bodies combine like nitroglycerin." She brought them over to an astrological chart on the wall. "Mars, Mercury, and Uranus are extreme influences. You see?" she said, pointing.

"Influences on what?" asked Mulder.

Zirinka put her hands in her pockets and smiled, like the cat who ate the canary. "Office hours are nine to five," she said. "All major credit cards accepted." She slipped a business card into Mulder's hand. He was not at all amused.

Chapter Seven

Many students at Grover Cleveland Alexander High School were obsessed with a yellow-eyed, yellow-horned beast. They would chant its praises, they would wear its image, they would keep it close to their hearts. It was painted in a giant circle in the center of the gymnasium. It was, of course, Googie the Goat, beloved mascot and team emblem of the Grover Cleveland Gruffs. On this particular afternoon, Googie was being trampled underfoot as the high school's basketball team brought the ball up and down court.

The cheerleaders sat on the sidelines, practicing unenthusiastic encouragements. No one was in the mood to be cheerful today, and Terri and Margi were no exception. They were delegated the task of dispensing sports drinks to the players. But since the coach allowed his players no relief, their efforts were in vain.

They sat bored and listless behind a card table covered with at least a hundred cups which they had already filled. With all the recent excitement in town, their cheerleading responsibilities seemed pathetically dull to them. So as they sat there, they played their favorite game: Hunk Critic.

The ball came flying over their heads, and Craig Wilmore ran past them to retrieve it, the heavy musk of his sweat wafting out behind him.

"What do we give Craig Wilmore?" Terri asked Margi.

Margi gave an immediate thumbs-down. "Hate him. He's totally deodorant deficient."

Terri waffled a bit, wrinkling her nose as he breezed past again and back into the game. "You're right," said Terri. "But I'll give him points for improved dermatology. A reluctant thumbs-up."

At center court a fight broke out. Two of the players bumped each other in the chest, like animals butting heads, and then began swinging at one another. Margi and Terri watched, detached and disgusted.

"Can it be true that these people will be adults before long, bringing life into the world?" asked Margi.

Terri shook her head in disbelief. "I'm *so* depressed."

It took four other guys and a coach to break up the fight. One of the players took the opportunity to grab a drink from the girls' table. It was Scott Simmons, arguably the best-looking player on the basketball team. He downed the whole cup in front of them. The girls could practically feel his body heat pulsating like an aura.

"Hi, Scott," said Terri with a coy smile. Scott crumpled his cup and flipped them a smile from the corner of his mouth, before jogging back toward the court. Terri leaned closer to Margi. "Our rating for Scott Simmons?" Terri asked as they checked out every last inch of him as he moved away.

"Babe-alicious in overtime," said Margi. "Thumbs *way* up!"

"Ditto," said Terri. "Uh, minus the *Brenda* appendage, of course."

Scott hadn't gone back to the game yet. Instead, he made a pit stop on the other end of the cheerleading squad, to sneak a kiss with his girlfriend, the oh-so-perfect Brenda Jaycee Summerfield. Brenda was sweet, made good grades, and had the kind of body that high-school boys were obsessed with. She had hogged all the cute boys since seventh grade. As far as Terri and Margi were concerned, it didn't matter how many popularity contests she won. Top-heavy Brenda was just an accident waiting to happen.

"Hate her!" said Terri.

"Hate her. Wouldn't want to date her," said Margi, completing a rhyme that they had shared since elementary school.

Brenda was clapping happily as Scott re-entered the game—when unexpectedly her feet flew out from under her and she landed squarely on her aerobically maintained butt. The girls next to her helped her up. Terri and Margi simply watched from the other end of the gym.

"Ooh—bad landing," mumbled Margi with a grin. "That'll cost her at least a tenth of a point."

"Dangerous place to land," said Terri. "Hope she didn't hurt her *brains*!"

They laughed over that, never noticing the disaster approaching from their blind spot. Without warning, their card table was broadsided and a sports drink explosion knocked them off their feet. One of the players, Eric Bauer, had chased an errant pass—right into them. The table flew, the drinks flew, the girls flew. When they got up, they were sticky and wet from the light-green sports drink that now covered them from head to toe.

"Oh! Hey—sorry," said Eric. And then the coach called him back into the game. He shrugged, and trotted off.

"*Hate* him," growled Terri.

"*Hate* him," echoed Margi, "wouldn't want

to *date* him."

They focused all of their attention on Eric Bauer. Although no one else noticed it, the spilled fluid on the floor around them began to boil.

Eric Bauer couldn't help grinning just the slightest bit, to see the witchy little debutantes completely soaked. For as long as he'd known Margi and Terri, they had been their own private little clique. The two of them spent all of their time together, finding unpleasant things to say about people behind their backs. From the time Eric Bauer was a kid, they had called him "Bow-wow"—so much so that the other kids had picked up the nickname all the way through junior high. No, Eric Bauer had never liked Margi and Terri, and seeing them all wet was satisfaction— small though it was.

His reverie was broken by a ball to the head. He turned to see who had thrown it to him, but there was no one there.

"Sorry, man," said Scott Simmons, "I was

passing it to Joe." That didn't seem right, because Joe was clear in the other direction. It was as if the ball had made a right turn in midair, just to hit Eric. Weird.

The ball bounced off and rolled underneath the bleachers. The rule was whoever was last to touch it had to go get it. So Eric took it upon himself to retrieve it.

He squeezed his way through the narrow opening between the tall wooden bleachers, weaving his way around steel support beams. The ball was against the back wall. He batted away the cobwebs underneath the bleachers. The second his fingers touched the ball . . .

. . . the lights went out.

"Hey! What gives?" he said. He could hear the voices of the other players echoing on the court in irritation. A couple of backup security lights snapped on, but they were of little help to Eric, still stuck beneath the bleachers.

Then he heard the grinding of gears.

BAM! At the far end of the gym, the first set of bleachers suddenly slammed back to the wall. The few spectators sitting on it plunged to the floor with sudden shouts.

At first, Eric was just confused. "What the . . . ?"

BAM! The second set of bleachers accordioned back to the wall, with the same bone-crushing speed and earsplitting noise. It was impossible—the machine simply didn't work that fast!

BAM! The third set of bleachers flew back with such force that its wood splintered in all directions. The wall behind it cracked.

Eric was behind the fifth set of bleachers. He dropped the ball.

"HEEELLLLP!" he screamed. "*Somebody stop it! Help me!*" He began to run through the maze of iron, bumping his arms and legs on the metal and wood around him, trying to squeeze between the bars.

BAM! The fourth set of bleachers smashed into the wall, sending a puff of dusty air into his face. He heard the bleachers around him start to move. He dove for it.

BAM! The bleachers pulled back, practically exploding as they hit the wall. Eric had made it under the sixth row of bleachers just in time . . . but he suddenly realized he hadn't made it out entirely. His hand had been caught. He'd felt a sudden crunch but didn't feel any pain—not yet, anyway. When he glanced back, he saw his smashed hand trapped in the metal of the fifth bleacher. He couldn't feel his fingers, and he thought he saw a couple of them on the floor. He couldn't think about that right now. He was beneath the sixth bleacher, just a few feet from freedom. But try as he might, he couldn't pull his ruined hand free. He could only stand there and scream, as metal and wood began to hurtle toward him and the bleachers flattened themselves against the wall. He felt pressure cutting into his legs, his gut, his chest.

And finally, as he heard the shattering of his own skull, he felt nothing at all.

Chapter Eight

It was nearly midnight. Scully was just considering a nice, hot bath to help her get to sleep, when the motel-room phone rang. It was Detective White.

"There's been another death," she reported.

"Where?" Scully asked.

"The high-school gymnasium."

"Right. I'll get Mulder," Scully said.

There was a pause at the other end of the line. "Um . . . he's already here," Detective White said, offering Scully no explanation.

When Scully arrived at the gym, she saw a group of police officers interviewing the boys on the basketball team, the girls on the cheerleading squad, and a few other witnesses. There were two police photographers snapping pictures of the scene, and a group of restless paramedics apparently waiting for some cue to do their jobs.

And across the room, near the closed bleachers, she saw Mulder with that woman.

Mulder was peering under the locked stands, trying to see something hidden in the dark recesses. A work crew, with crowbars and wrenches, was struggling to open the set of bleachers next to him. As Scully got closer, she saw the pool of blood seeping onto the gym floor near their feet.

"What happened?" she asked briskly.

Detective White, who hadn't seen her approach, jumped at the sound of her voice. Mulder turned to see Scully, and straightened up.

"From what we've been able to gather, there was a power surge. It caused all the lights to go out but also somehow activated the motor that opens and closes these bleachers. The victim was trapped inside."

Scully couldn't help grimacing at the horror of this death.

Another police officer approached them. "Detective White, we need you for a moment."

"Excuse me," she said, and joined a gaggle of arguing policemen across the room. Detective White seemed to be trying to mediate, but instead became caught up in the argument herself.

It seemed to Scully that everyone here was having similar difficulties. The officers interviewing the frightened witnesses were argumentative and harsh, making the process more difficult than necessary. The two photographers seemed to be getting in each other's way. Even the workers trying to free the bleachers couldn't agree on an approach.

Scully watched the workmen for a little while longer. Mulder stared at the pool of blood on the floor, as if trying to discern an answer from the puddle.

"Why weren't you in your motel room?" Scully asked him at last.

"I was with Detective White," Mulder explained. Then, realizing how that might be interpreted, he went on. "We were following up on a lead."

"I see." Scully snorted.

"You see *what?*" Mulder asked, annoyed.

Scully turned to face him. "Look," she said, knowing that every bit of the weariness she felt was showing in her voice. "We've been working together now for how many years? We have differing opinions about this case. Okay, that happens. But I didn't expect you to ditch me."

Mulder laughed. "I didn't ditch you."

Scully turned away. She didn't want to debate this now. Especially not at a crime scene. And certainly not with a young man lying dead just a few feet away.

"Fine," she said. "Whatever."

Just then, the workmen freed the jammed bleacher and pulled it open.

The paramedics moved in at last to recover the crushed body.

The witnesses had long ago gone home. Only the two FBI agents and the police team remained. It was nearly dawn when they left the gym.

Outside, Mulder said good-bye to Detective White, and Scully nodded a curt acknowledgment. But by the time they had walked to their car, Detective White called them back.

They trudged over to her car, where she was just hanging up the handset to her police radio.

"We've got trouble," she said, looking up at them. "A mob has gathered on the south side of town."

Scully and Mulder glanced at each other. There would be no rest for them this night, no matter how weary they were.

Chapter Nine

The sun was just rising when Scully and Mulder, following Detective White's car and several police cruisers, pulled up to an open field behind a residential neighborhood.

Several dozen people were hard at work in the field, digging for all they were worth. If Scully didn't know better, she would say this looked like a simple community project—as though the townsfolk were digging an irrigation ditch, or preparing an Easter egg hunt. But she feared this was a far less innocent endeavor.

As they got out of the car, Scully recognized several of the shovel-wielding men and women from the funeral service the day before. She even thought she saw Jay DeBoom's parents.

One man, facing away from them, seemed to be in charge of the entire operation. He was assigning places for people to dig; then he waved to the driver of a backhoe to move in. As the mud-covered work machine rumbled forward, lowering its huge yellow bucket, the leader of the mob turned around. Scully recognized him immediately.

It was the wild-eyed man who had disrupted the funeral service yesterday. He saw the law-enforcement officers and strode forward to greet them.

Detective White confronted him.

"What's going on here, Bob?" she asked him, barely masking her frustration. It was clear from her attitude that the last thing she wanted was for this unruly mob to interfere with her orderly police investigation.

Bob's wild eyes were ablaze. "George Hunsaker's little boy got a phone call from someone who gave us the location of the mass grave!"

"You can't do this, Bob," she said flatly. "You're going to have to stop digging."

"Our children are dying!" the man cried in response.

But Detective White shook her head. "It doesn't give you the right to come out here and tear up Harvey Molitch's backyard."

The corners of Bob's mouth twitched into a triumphant smile. "We have his permission," he said, gesturing to a nearby group of men. One of them, an overweight man in bib overalls, sheepishly waved at Detective White.

She looked at him and shook her head. "Harvey Molitch," she said, "this is all right with you?"

The man nodded, mopping at some perspiration on his brow. "Oh, yeah," Molitch said. "If there's a mass grave on my property, I guess I oughta know about it. Wouldn't want people to think I put it there."

The men standing next to Harvey looked at him suspiciously.

Detective White threw up her hands and let them fall limply to her sides. "Fine," she said. "Do whatever you want."

Wild-eyed Bob nodded in agreement. "Yeah," he said fiercely, "we will." Then he actually cackled before he went back to supervising the dig.

"That man," Mulder asked, indicating the leader. "Is he always this hysterical?"

Detective White shook her head sadly. "No. Bob Spitz is our high-school principal. He's about the most levelheaded person in town . . . until recently, that is."

Scully, standing behind them, spoke up. "It's called rumor panic."

Mulder and Detective White turned to her.

"There have been at least twenty incidents since 1983," Scully continued, "from Upstate New York to Reno, Nevada. An event, like the deaths of the high-school boys, linked with horrific cult myths increases tension in a community, straining it to the breaking point."

Mulder nodded at Scully. Perhaps she was finally getting through to him. Maybe he was ready to concede that she just might be right about this case.

Scully looked around at the men and women who were frantically churning up the field. She nodded. "Yes. This is a textbook case. Of course, not once has a shred of evidence turned up to support any of the wild accusations—"

Scully was interrupted by the shouts of a woman halfway across the field. "I found bones!"

"We found bones!" yelled Bob Spitz, pointing.

"We found bones! We found bones!" came the echoes from around the field.

Mulder glanced at Scully. "There's always a first time." He turned and followed Detective White to the location of the original shout.

Scully tightened her mouth into a grim line and followed, gingerly picking her way through the pockmarked field.

Police officers had formed a ring around the hole, holding back the indignant, angry crush. They allowed only Detective White, Mulder, and Scully to approach.

At the bottom of the shallow pit a leather bag lay, half-covered in dirt. The metal clasp between the two handles was unfastened, the bag slightly open.

"They're in the bag," said the woman who had been digging there.

Stooping by the side of the hole, Scully could see something white inside the bag, but she couldn't make out what it was. She reached into her pocket and pulled out a pair of latex gloves. Even though the bag had been buried for who knows how long, they might still be able to lift a few finger-prints off it.

She glanced over and saw Mulder, crouching next to her, also fumbling with a pair of gloves.

They looked at each other for an awkward moment; then Mulder began putting his gloves away.

"Go ahead," he said, scowling.

"No," Scully said, more bothered by his

attitude than she should have been. "You go ahead."

"Oh, no," Mulder insisted, the gloves already back in his pocket. "Be my guest." He looked at her evenly. "I know how much you like snapping on the latex."

Scully glared at Mulder as she pulled on the gloves, exaggerating the snap at the end. Reaching into the hole, she hauled out the leather bag by one of its handles.

It had the unmistakable shape of a doctor's bag. Scully deposited it on the ground and pulled it open. Sure enough, she could see the bag was filled with tiny bones.

So could Bob Spitz, who had somehow skirted around the police line and was staring into the bag over Scully's and Mulder's shoulders.

"They're a child's bones!" he cried. The crowd answered with a roar of horror and approval.

Scully looked to Detective White for help. "Detective, please!"

Detective White nodded at the officers,

and they pulled Bob Spitz back outside their cordoned-off area. Still he pressed forward as far as he could, straining to catch every word.

Scully took another look at the bones as she gently shook the bag. The skull was shattered beyond recognition. She'd have to check the bones when she got back to the police station. *They could be human*, she thought. *Maybe . . .* but she wasn't convinced. In any case, she didn't want to say anything just yet, for fear of inciting the crowd.

Mulder, looking at the outside of the leather case, pointed at a brass oval covered with crusted earth. "Do you see this lettering?" he asked. "It looks like a monogram."

Scully brushed away some of the dirt with a gloved finger. " 'R. W. G.' ," she read.

Mulder turned to Detective White. "Angela," he said, "do you know who R. W. G. might be?"

But before she could answer, Bob Spitz cried out, "Dick Godfrey!" He turned to the crowd and screamed, "That bag belonged to

Dr. Godfrey! He's the baby killer!"

The crowd reacted instantly. Without a word of consultation or planning, they turned together and rushed for their cars.

Detective White and the two FBI agents stood, watching them go, powerless to stop them.

"Angela, who's Dr. Godfrey?" Mulder asked.

"He's our town pediatrician," the detective answered.

Mulder and Scully started trotting after the retreating mob.

But in spite of the urgency of the situation, and the danger that now faced Dr. Godfrey, all Scully found herself thinking was, *Oh, so now he's calling her Angela . . .*

Chapter Ten

The angry mob stormed from their cars toward Dr. Godfrey's house like a mass of incensed townsfolk storming Dracula's castle. They crowded onto his porch. Bob Spitz pounded on the door, its glass panes rattling violently under his heavy fist.

Clearly the good doctor was not expecting visitors on this particular morning. The fact of the matter was that since his wife had passed away several years ago, he found her clothes—which were still in the closet—a pleasant reminder of her. Which might explain why he came racing down the stairs wearing her nightgown, her slippers, and her perfume—but then again, it might not.

In any case, the doctor came racing down the stairs, and as soon as he saw the shadows of the crowd behind the thin curtains, he raced back up to dress himself a bit more presentably.

He was only half finished when he heard the window downstairs breaking and the door being forced. He heard dozens of feet pounding up the stairs. He tried to call the police, but the mob crashed through his bedroom door before he could dial. He barely recognized Bob Spitz, whose eyes seemed to retain only a tiny remnant of sanity. His friends and neighbors—people he had once trusted—now screamed vile, vicious things at him. Before he knew what was happening, he was forced down the stairs and out the door, caught in the unforgiving arms of the frenzied mob.

Dr. Godfrey, now wearing a white shirt and navy slacks, sat with his eyes turned down in the interrogation room of the Comity jail. His hands were clasped tightly in front of him, resting on the interrogation-room table. Having been rescued by the police from what was sure to be an old-fashioned lynching, he was almost more relieved than he was frightened.

"Let me get this straight," said Detective White, sitting across the table from him. "For the record. You haven't seen the bag for years—since you sold it at a garage sale."

Dr. Godfrey nodded, a short, nervous jerk of his head. "Yes," he said haltingly, "that's right. To a young girl. Terri Roberts. Had to have been five, six years ago."

Mulder, his hands in his pockets, stood behind Detective White. Now he walked around the table and sat on the edge of it, looking down at the suspect. "Why would it be filled with bones and buried in a field?"

Dr. Godfrey seemed to be on the verge of tears. "I don't know," he said, his voice shaking. "I have no idea."

Mulder believed him. In his experience, few liars could answer so convincingly. But Detective White wasn't through with him yet.

"Would you be willing to take a lie-detector test?" she asked.

Dr. Godfrey nodded. "Yes," he whispered. "Anything—"

But it would not be necessary.

Scully breezed into the interrogation room and dropped the bag in question onto the table. "You can go now, Dr. Godfrey," she said. "I don't think we'll be needing anything more from you."

Detective White turned and glared at her. "Now wait just a—"

But Scully just smiled briskly and continued to address the pediatrician. "Your story checked out."

Dr. Godfrey didn't need to be told twice. "Oh, thank you," he said, standing and taking a few steps back from the table. "Thank you."

Mulder, now standing in front of Dr. Godfrey, looked at his partner expectantly as she placed the doctor's old bag on the interrogation-room table and pulled it open.

"As I suspected," she said, sounding very satisfied with herself, "the bones were not those of a human infant. They're the remains of a beloved Lhasa apso, formerly known as"—she reached into the bag and produced a thin leather dog collar, turning the tag for him to see—" 'Mr. Tippy.' "

As if on cue, a police officer opened the door and Terri Roberts entered the interrogation room. When she saw the aged medical bag on the table and the collar in Scully's hands, tears filled her eyes.

"Oh, Mr. Tippy," she said. The girl walked over to Scully, who placed a tender hand on her shoulder as she handed her the collar. Terri burst into tears.

Mulder, suddenly distracted from the sad little drama, glanced from Detective White to Scully and back again. "This might not be the best time to mention it," Mulder said, "but someone is wearing my favorite perfume."

Dr. Godfrey jumped slightly and quickly moved to the door, where his jacket was hanging on a peg. "Well, I'll just be going," he said, hurriedly putting his arms through the sleeves.

Scully simply looked at her partner, and said, "Can I have a word with you?"

The two of them left the interrogation room together, and walked a few paces down the hall.

Finally Scully spun around to face Mulder. All the fury that had been building inside her needed release. She managed to hold on for one more moment as the curiously fragrant Dr. Godfrey passed, and then she let Mulder have it.

"This has gone far enough," she seethed.

Mulder looked at her, plainly baffled. It wasn't just that he didn't know what she was talking about. He wasn't even able to focus on her words. He was still thinking about the wonderful scent of his favorite perfume.

"What?" he asked.

Scully was tired of being ignored by her partner. Tears welled up in her eyes. Her words poured out in a torrent.

"Ever since we got here I've put up with your snide comments and your patronizing attitude," Scully said. "Well, I'm not going to be humiliated by you anymore, and—" It was all she could do not to pound his chest with her fist as she went on: "And I'm not going to bring a teenage girl in—on her birthday, of all days—to identify the bones of her dead dog, Mr. Tippy!"

All Mulder heard was an unpleasant burst of emotion-laden gibberish. The only thing that interested him—the thing he was suddenly, inexplicably, obsessed by—was figuring out which woman was wearing his favorite scent.

He leaned forward and gently sniffed the air around Scully.

Scully didn't seem to notice. She was caught up in her own harangue and was determined to make her point. "I find no reason to pursue this case any further. Not only that, I find your conduct in this investigation not just alarming but highly objectionable!"

Mulder had his nose very close to her forehead now, and he sniffed again.

"What are you doing?" she snapped.

Mulder shook his head. "It must be Angela," he murmured softly.

Scully looked at her partner with undisguised contempt. "If that's the reason we're sticking around," she said finally, "then that's your business. Not mine."

She turned and walked quickly down the hall.

Mulder finally realized that Scully was upset, although he also realized he had no idea why.

"What?" he asked, following after her.

Scully stopped suddenly and turned, and Mulder stopped short, almost thrown off balance.

Scully looked him in the eye and said, "Detective White. Detective *Angela* White."

Mulder looked at her, searching. What was she getting at? What was the last thing they had said to each other? "Scully," Mulder began, then plunged ahead, hoping his words made sense in the context of their conversation, "we came down here because of three unexplained deaths. Detective White is just trying to solve them. She can use our help."

"Well," Scully said, obviously still upset, "you two seem to have developed a certain . . .

rapport. So good luck with the case. *I'm* going back to Washington in the morning."

With that, she walked away.

"Scully!" Mulder called after her. But she didn't turn around, didn't even slow down.

Mulder watched her go. Part of him wanted to say, Fine, good riddance. But . . . he would *never* say something like that to Scully, would he?

He was about to chase after Scully to tell her what he had just realized . . .

. . . when he caught a lingering trace of perfume in the air, and forgot about everything but tracking down the scent.

Chapter Eleven

The celestial syzygy was due to occur precisely at midnight.

At seven o'clock in the evening, exactly five hours short of that, Margi, Terri, and a group of their friends participated in a uniquely human ritual: They celebrated the girls' birthday. Of course, they hadn't quite turned eighteen yet—that wouldn't happen until the stroke of midnight. In fact, they were born closer together than twins could be—delivered exactly eighteen years ago in adjacent hospital rooms at precisely the same moment. It was that strange bond that had made their families friends. Who could blame the girls for being closer than sisters?

Their birthday-party guest list had included the entire cheerleading squad, some obligatory cousins, and a select sampling of the boys in school. None of the invited boys showed up. Several of them were dead—and as for the rest, they had suddenly developed an instinctive discomfort, and even fear, around the girls that they couldn't explain.

"It's been a bad month," Margi's mother tried to console her, when it appeared that all the guests had arrived with not a male face in the bunch. "With all that's going on, it's hard for people to go to parties, dear."

But that was fine with Terri and Margi, who really weren't interested in their birthday anyway. They had teased out their hair like psychotic birds of prey and obsessively brushed on makeup until their faces were barely recognizable beneath the layers of color. Then, when the boys didn't show, they cranked up the music and danced together—just the two of them, with wild, primal gyrations, like those in a tribal rite. The other girls just watched and gaped, sitting like wallflowers around the room. But Margi and Terri didn't notice, and didn't care.

It was halfway through the party that someone dug out an old Ouija board. The guests entertained themselves with prognostications while Terri and Margi continued to dance madly in the center of the room. Even so, they could hear the questions their guests were asking the Ouija board, and they were more than happy to oblige with answers.

When Betty Jo Sloat asked what her career would be, the Ouija wand flew across the board, its little eye spelling out G-R-A-V-E-D-I-G-G-E-R.

When Roxy Sherman asked where she would go to college, the answer came back S-E-W-E-R-U.

But the best, by far, was Brenda Jaycee Summerfield, who asked, "Who am I going to marry?"

All of the girls were most attentive to this question, because as everyone knew, Brenda and Scott Simmons had passed the test of time—so far, they'd gone out for two whole months. Brenda put her fingertips to the Ouija planchette, and it drew her fingers across the table in a circle, until its eye settled over the letter S. Brenda grinned at her friends knowingly. Next the planchette shot across the board, stopping, surprisingly, on the letter A. And then, without meandering in the least, it shot to the letter T, then to the letter A again, and then ended on the letter N.

"Satan," all the girls mumbled in unison, looking at one another, afraid to say anything more.

Brenda burst into tears and ran out of the room. The rest of the girls sat in nervous silence. Their hostesses were nowhere to be seen.

Terri and Margi had slipped off together to await Brenda's arrival, once the name of her husband-to-be was spelled out.

Brenda entered the bathroom brushing tears from her eyes, as they knew she would. Terri and Margi were standing in front of the mirror—their hair as wild as demons', their eyes glowing and dilated like the eyes of a cat. Together they chanted:

"One Bloody Mary, two Bloody Mary, three Bloody Mary . . ."

"Wha . . . what are you two doing?" Brenda

asked apprehensively. They turned on her in unison.

"You just close your eyes and count to thirteen," said Margi, "and Bloody Mary appears in the mirror." Her voice was as smooth as wet ice—her smile as jagged as broken glass.

"Why don't you try it, Brenda," said Terri.

Brenda shook her head and started to back away. "No." But the door suddenly slammed behind her, and the two birthday girls turned back to the mirror and began counting again:

". . . four Bloody Mary, five Bloody Mary, six Bloody Mary . . ."

Out in the living room, the guests were still staring at the Ouija board. The planchette rested on the N. No one dared to move it or even touch it. Around them the music blared screeching guitars and screeching voices. But the stereophonics of the screams seemed a little bit off.

One of the screaming voices was not coming from the speakers at all.

Quickly, Betty Jo Sloat ran to turn off the

stereo. The screams were coming from some-where in the house, along with the sounds of shattering glass. They raced off to find Brenda.

It was Betty Jo who found her. "Oh, my God," Betty Jo whispered, and then she could not stop screaming.

"What's wrong, Betty?" asked Carrie Richards before she saw it too.

Brenda was lying on a bathroom floor that had once been white and was now a deep liquid red.

The mirror had shattered, but there were few shards on the floor.

Somehow most of the shards had been absorbed by the almost unrecognizable body on the floor.

Brenda, pretty Brenda, was a bloody human pincushion.

The girls screamed and screamed.

And Margi and Terri were nowhere to be seen.

Chapter Twelve

Mulder sat alone in his room at the Comity Motel holding a pint bottle of vodka.

Which was unusual, because he almost never drank. Certainly not alone.

After Scully had left him at the jail, taking the car with her, Mulder had decided to walk back to the motel rather than call a cab.

On the way he passed a liquor store. This one, like the one they had seen as they'd headed into town, also had a line that snaked out to the sidewalk. Mulder found himself standing in line with the rest of the townsfolk. But it wasn't what you would call a festive, friendly crowd. In fact, Mulder didn't say a word for nearly twenty minutes, until he finally reached the front of the line. And when the man at the counter asked him what he wanted, he realized he had no idea. He just asked for the same thing the man before him had asked for.

Mulder took another sip of the vodka. Rotgut—isn't that what they called stuff like this? *If Satan really was here*, Mulder idly thought, *he'd be in this little bottle.*

After he had reached the motel, Mulder had gone straight to his room and sat down in this chair. And never moved. Gradually, so gradually he hadn't even noticed, it became dark outside.

In that time the town outside seemed to be going crazy. He heard voices raised in heated argument, the sounds of squealing brakes, and so many sirens he had lost count.

Dimly he wondered about Scully. He hoped she was taking care of herself, wherever she was. He took another pull on the bottle.

As it happened, Scully was just a few yards away, in her own motel room.

She sat on the chair next to her bed and

took another drag from her cigarette. Which, when she thought about it, was truly strange. She hadn't so much as taken a single puff on a cigarette since college, having had brains enough to quit before she became a slave to tobacco. She didn't know what had possessed her to buy a pack when she was in the convenience store. Maybe it was just to spite the surgeon general's smug little warning.

She looked in disgust at the cigarette nestled between her fingers. Then she mashed it out in the ashtray and picked up the remote control.

An old black-and-white film appeared on the TV. *The Keystone Kops.* Scully watched the scratchy old film for a few moments. An old-time paddy wagon was piled high with the ridiculous Kops. They hung on for dear life as the vehicle careened down the street, narrowly missing car after car, losing the occasional Kop as it spun at full speed around a corner.

Scully had never cared much for slapstick, and right now the movie only made her more depressed. The Keystone Kops' ineptness served only to remind her of how she and Mulder were stumbling around in this case without a clue. She clicked the remote to change the channel. But the image didn't change. The Keystone Kops, with their long black coats, droopy mustaches, and tall round hats, were still bumbling about on her screen.

Absently lighting another cigarette, she changed the channel again. Again the number in the upper left-hand corner of the screen changed. And again the image didn't.

Finally she just turned the TV off.

She stood up and began to pace, replaying her last conversation with Mulder in her mind, and taking a long, deep drag from her cigarette.

Mulder stared at his TV set, uncomprehending.

After sitting for he didn't know how long, he had finally turned on the TV. With the vodka bottle in one hand and the remote in the other, he discovered the same absurd broadcasts that had bedeviled Scully.

No matter which channel he switched to, the only thing the tube had to offer was *The Keystone Kops*.

"There's never anything good on," he slurred, tossing the remote onto the bed.

He heard a series of soft knocks at the door and strode over to look through the peephole.

It was Detective White. Through the fish-eye lens of the peephole, Mulder could see she was holding a white box.

And that she had been crying.

Mulder straightened up and opened the door. They looked at each other across the threshold, neither daring to make the first move.

"May I come in?" Angela asked meekly.

Mulder nodded, and moved aside. Leaving the door slightly ajar, he turned to face her. "What's wrong?" he asked.

"I . . . I found this on my front doorstep," she managed to get out as she handed him the box.

Mulder sat down on the bed and lifted the lid.

Inside the box, resting on a bed of flowers, was the collar he had last seen around the neck of Detective White's cat.

Mulder looked up as the woman burst into tears. "If they aren't satanists," she sobbed, "then who are they?"

Mulder went to her then and put his arms around her. It was a natural human response, after all. But as they held each other, Mulder had an urge to do more. An uncontrollable desire to . . .

. . . smell her perfume.

He had to acknowledge that his relationship with Detective White had become somewhat closer than the ones he usually established with the local police authorities. In fact, he saw this embrace as a sign of their newly defined closeness.

Detective White suddenly spoke up, breaking the spell. "I don't really want to go home. Would you mind if I slept here?"

Mulder was puzzled. Was Angela actually proposing to stay here—with him? "I can get you another room . . . or, if you really want this room, I'll get another . . ."

Detective White didn't answer. She didn't have to. Because before Mulder knew what was happening, they both suddenly fell onto the bed. Of course they were fully clothed, but as Detective White kissed him again and again, that fact seemed like a mere technicality.

The Keystone Kops were in the middle of an enormous pie fight, covered with whipped cream and waving their billy clubs madly, when Scully walked into Mulder's unlocked room.

"Mulder!"

Both Mulder and Detective White sat up to see Scully standing in the doorway. She was glaring at the two of them, with an expression triangulated somewhere between shock, anger, and hurt.

It would be difficult to catalog all the thoughts that went through Mulder's mind at this moment. So he tried not to. Instead he bounced off the bed, as if nothing were going on.

"There's been another death," Scully said in soft disgust, before leaving the room.

Detective White's face was ashen as she stood up.

They trotted after Scully, and caught up to her in the motel parking lot.

"Was it a murder?" Mulder asked. First things first.

"Hard to say," said Scully, coolly professional. "A high-school girl was impaled by flying glass from a bathroom mirror."

Detective White headed for her car, parked next to Mulder and Scully's rented one. Mulder took a few steps closer to Scully as she opened the driver's door.

"Let me drive," he said.

"I'm driving," she said firmly.

"Scully," Mulder said softly to her, "what happened in there—it's not what you think."

"It doesn't matter what I think," she said,

sliding behind the wheel.

"Will you let me drive, please?" Mulder asked, more insistently.

Scully clung to the wheel. Suddenly, driving this car meant a lot to her, beyond the obvious reasons. Somehow it seemed to represent everything about their relationship, professional and otherwise. "Why do you always have to drive?" she snapped. "Because you're the guy? Because you're the big macho man?"

"No," said Mulder, backing off, suddenly angrier than he should have been. "I was just never sure your little feet could reach the pedals."

Scully angrily slammed the door as Mulder walked over to Detective White, still standing next to her car. Mulder gently took the keys from her hand.

"Will you go with Agent Scully, please?"

Detective White shrugged, then walked to the car where Scully was fuming. Just as Detective White got into the passenger seat,

Scully floored the accelerator and tore out of the parking lot, turning left on the street to head toward the crime scene.

Mulder sat behind the wheel of Detective White's car and adjusted the rearview mirror, which still swam before his eyes. He turned the key in the ignition, angrily shoved the car into gear, and followed Scully as far as the driveway. But when he reached the street, he turned right and drove off in the opposite direction, joining the many weaving hordes of dangerously drunk drivers that careened through the suddenly psychotic town of Comity.

Chapter Thirteen

Terri and Margi had no desire to wallow in the unpleasant aftermath of their Bloody Mary extravaganza. They snuck out while the other girls were scrambling toward the bathroom, and ran down the street, laughing as they went.

The news spread quickly through town, in hushed whispers over phone lines: Brenda Summerfield was the latest teen killed by the mysterious cult. And now the birthday girls had vanished, too. Nobody knew what terrible thing might have happened to them.

It was after ten when they showed up at the local Banzai Burger, having tracked Scott Simmons down to the hamburger joint like bloodhounds. He sat there alone, behind an uneaten burger and a spread of greasy fries.

He was, in his own way, mourning the loss of "the Brenda appendage." As the birthday girls approached, they couldn't help finding his sad, puppy-dog eyes incredibly sexy. They sauntered directly up to him in their tight leather outfits and sat at the table without hesitation—forcing their way into his space.

"Hey," said Margi. "Bummer about Brenda, huh?"

Scott stared at them with those sad eyes, unable to speak. Terri looked down at his food. "Loss of appetite—that's not a good sign." She began to pick at his uneaten fries like a vulture picking over a carcass.

Scott looked at them incredulously. "Excuse me, but I'd like to be alone right now."

Terri shrugged and munched another fry. "Well, looks like you got your wish!"

Margi only stared at him, flinging her hair back suggestively.

Scott clearly couldn't believe what was going on in front of him. "What happened to you guys?" he said. "You used to be . . ."

"Look, Scott," said Terri, in no mood for small talk. "We're not dressed like this for the funeral. We're here to make you feel better—tonight. You know—'Carpe P.M.' "

Margi tossed her hair again. "Hey, girlfriend," said Margi. "That's 'Carpe D.M.' Don't you know your Spanish?" Terri shoved a french fry into Margi's mouth to shut her up, and giggled. When they turned back to Scott, he was looking at them like they were both crazy, which, of course, they were—a fact they both *knew* but didn't care about in the least. It simply felt too good to care. Too powerful.

Scott quickly slid out of the booth and stormed out of the restaurant. Terri shrugged and pulled his hamburger toward her.

"Hate him," she said flippantly, which lately had been a prelude to murder. When Margi didn't respond with the usual retort, Terri tried again, this time more emphatically: "*Hate him.*"

But Margi just stared at her defiantly, and left to follow Scott.

Terri's face contracted into a scowl, and

she took a deep bite into Scott's hamburger, like a lioness taking a chunk of zebra.

Several miles away, Scully and Detective White were driving toward the latest murder scene, both staring straight ahead, in intense, thick silence—when something hit the windshield with a *thud*.

Scully slammed on the brakes. The car fishtailed. She tried to regain control, but suddenly the ground became uneven and the vehicle began to buffet and shimmy as they rolled over objects in the road. Something hit the roof and bounced off. Then something splattered over the windshield—something bloody. They caught sight of a flutter of feathers and a small black eye peering in at them before the bird rolled onto the ground. Finally Scully managed to bring the car to a halt.

It seemed to be raining outside. But not water.

It was, in fact, raining birds. Hundreds of them.

Scully and Detective White stepped from

100

the car, and their jaws dropped in disbelief. Piles of birds littered the road. One more dropped from the heavens, landing with a *plop* on Detective White's shoulder. She grimaced, and brushed it off with a little yelp.

Scully refused to make a sound. She wasn't about to give Detective White the satisfaction of knowing that she was just as shocked. "Unusual weather," she said matter-of-factly, and knelt down to look at one of the birds, pulling back its wing. Its eyes had been pecked out and its body was full of long claw marks. "From the look of it," said Scully, "this flock of birds turned on itself. For some reason, they killed each other."

But Detective White suddenly had other things on her mind. "Agent Scully," she said, pointing. Scully looked up to see at least two dozen flashlights heading in their direction from down the road. A crowd of people marched toward them, ignoring the dead birds under their feet. In the moonlight, she could see the thin, metallic reflections on the shot-guns they were carrying. She began to wonder if the bodies of birds were the only thing that would be littering the streets tonight.

Mulder pounded on Zirinka's door for what seemed like hours. He knew she was there. He could hear the TV on upstairs. He would get her attention, even if he had to pound on her door all night. After a few more minutes of hard knocking, she finally came to the door.

"My hours are nine to five," she yelled, ready to slam the door in his face.

Mulder put his foot in the door. "How would you like to be brought in as a murder suspect?" he said. "Five teenagers, each more popular than the last. How would that look on your résumé, Zirinka?"

"I didn't have anything to do with it—you *know* that!"

Mulder smiled broadly. "Sure I do. But it won't stop me from making your life a living hell—and tonight I'd be happy to do just that."

Zirinka reluctantly pulled the door open for him, but still stood in his way. "Are you always this pleasant, Agent Mulder?"

"Actually," said Mulder, "I'm usually a pretty nice guy—but I'm in rare form tonight." And he pushed his way past her, into her fortune-telling salon. He handed her his credit card—business *was* business. Zirinka ran it through her machine and sat down, taking her own sweet time.

"Let's go already," said Mulder.

"I'm just waiting for the authorization," said Zirinka.

"Look! I'm a federal agent!"

"Last I heard, the federal government couldn't pay its bills."

Finally the machine beeped through an approval, and Zirinka examined the little blue letters on the LED screen. "Okay. You're good for up to three hundred bucks." She turned to Mulder with a sly smile. "Now, how can I help you?"

Mulder leaned his hands on her desk, looking straight at her. "You said you knew why people were behaving strangely here in Comity."

Zirinka smirked. "Yeah—the same reason my dog's been trying to mate with my gas barbecue for the last three weeks."

Mulder glanced up at the star chart behind her. "You said it was planetary . . ."

Zirinka nodded, and began to rattle off the information as if it was something she dealt with every day—which, apparently, it was.

"Once every eighty-four years," she began, "Mercury, Mars, and Uranus come into conjunction—but this year it's different, because Uranus is in the house of Aquarius."

"And that's a bad thing?"

Zirinka laughed. "Bad? Yeah, bad like a Stephen King movie. Things are going to fall from the sky, and there'll be disaster around every corner—especially in *this* town."

"What makes this place so special?"

Zirinka moved to a globe at the corner of her desk. It wasn't your typical globe—it was covered with astrological symbols and lines that meant nothing to Mulder. Zirinka spun the globe, then stopped it. She had her finger on a certain area of the United States where quite a few of those strange lines converged in a cluster. At the dead center was the small town of Comity.

"We're in a geological vortex," explained Zirinka, "a high-intensity meridian; a cosmic nerve center. All culminating at midnight on January twelfth, when the planets come into perfect alignment." She glanced at her watch. "Which, wonder of wonders, is tonight!"

"And this is affecting everyone," said Mulder. It was more a statement of fact than a question.

"It affects everyone to an extent—some people more than others. In general, relationships are going to suffer, inhibitions are going to be suppressed. A person's conscience can shut down completely. It all depends on the significant dates in that person's life. You see, key dates can exaggerate the effects."

"So," said Mulder, beginning to piece things together, "what if today was someone's birthday?"

Zirinka smiled. "Then I'd say, 'happy birthday.'" She paused. "Unless, of course, you were born in 1979. Then I'd call the police."

Mulder narrowed his eyes at her. "And why is that?"

Zirinka shrugged. "You'd have a Jupiter-Uranus opposition, forming what is called a Grand Square. That's when all the planets are aligned in a cross." And then she considered the severity of the situation—perhaps for the first time. "All the energy of the cosmos would be focused . . . on you."

"And that's a bad thing?" asked Mulder.

"Let's just say," said Zirinka, "I wouldn't want to be anywhere near this person . . . and I'd lock up my gas barbecue, as well."

Chapter Fourteen

Scott Simmons had a headache. He didn't want to think. He didn't want to *deal*. He just wanted to get home, go to sleep, and hope that the morning brought something better than today. He drove his pickup into his garage, hopped out, and clicked the electronic garage-door opener. The garage door came down to the ground behind him, hitting the concrete with a final *bang*.

"You don't have to be alone tonight," said a soft voice behind him. Scott jumped. He spun to see someone climbing out of the bed of his pickup. Someone with wild hair. Someone with tight leather clothes.

It was one of the birthday girls.

"Margi, what are you doing here?" Scott managed to squawk out.

Margi came toward him—too close for comfort. "Terri's insensitivity to your pain was just too much for me to bear," she whispered, leaning in to kiss him gently. "So I—"

"So you *what?*" came a voice beside them. Terri had just burst in through the side door of the garage. Even in silhouette, Scott could see her wild eyes, and the static sparking in her snarly hair. "So you blew me off to snag some shoulder time with Rude Boy?" Terri stormed toward them.

"Back off, Terri!" growled Margi in a voice that didn't even sound like hers. Terri stopped in her tracks and lowered her head, staring wickedly at her best friend.

"Happy birthday!" Terri said.

Scott could feel an unnatural tension in the air. He wanted to get out, to get away from them. Then he heard something from the corner of the garage . . .

One of the large garage-door springs had begun to vibrate and shake wildly. Suddenly it vanished, flying across the garage too fast for the human eye to see.

BANG!

The rear window of Scott's pickup exploded with the impact. The garage filled with the sound of fracturing glass, and then the final *twang*, as the two-foot spring vibrated to a stop, wedged deep in the dashboard.

Scott had no idea what he was witnessing. His brain was not quite ready to process what he had just seen, but he *did* know that he was in danger.

He watched as Margi lowered her head and focused her eyes on Terri with the same evil intensity.

"Right back at you," Margi said.

That's when Scott's instincts took over. He raced for the door—just as he heard the *twang* of the second spring.

Margi and Terri both ducked as it came firing past their heads. When they straightened, their eyes were still locked in a malevolent, fire-and-ice gaze—until they noticed something about each other.

"You're bleeding," said Terri, looking at the spots of blood speckled on Margi's face.

109

"So are you," said Margi, noticing the bloody spray in Terri's hair. It took only a moment to realize that the blood had not come from them. They turned simultaneously. Scott Simmons was standing against the wall, his eyes frozen in shock and disbelief. In the space where his belly button should have been protruded the end of the spring—still *twanging* itself silent.

He gurgled and then fell forward. The two-foot spring had gone straight through him and was imbedded at least a foot into the cinder-block wall.

"You killed him!" said Margi, shocked in spite of herself. She felt her own conscience struggling to wake up.

"What do you mean, *I* killed him?" said Terri. "*You* killed him!"

Margi knelt down beside the dead boy, staring at the hole in his back. She tried to make herself feel the horror she knew she *ought* to feel. But all she could think was that now all of the handsome boys in school were dead. The only ones left were dweebs. She knew her thinking was *wrong*; she knew she should be feeling something else right now. But somehow she couldn't figure out what that should be.

She turned to see that Terri had gone. "Terri?" She could hear her footsteps running into the night. Then, all at once, Margi did find a thought to hold on to.

Terri.

This was Terri's fault.

Yes. Yes, it had all been Terri's fault!

Terri ran down the street into the darkness, putting distance between herself and Margi. And as she ran, part of her sanity began to come back to her—a sanity that returned only when the two girls were apart.

All the horrible things that had happened, all the deaths . . . why, they had all been Margi's fault, hadn't they? Even though both she and Margi had sent the first boy's car off the cliff together, it was Margi's doing. Even though it was *her* hands that had helped drown Bruno, didn't *Margi* prompt that too?

And even though Terri was the one who put the rope around Jay DeBoom's neck, *Margi* was the one who had thought of using that rope. No, she could not accept the blame. It was Margi, always Margi.

And so Terri ran, not even knowing where she was running.

Chapter Fifteen

Zirinka handed Mulder back his credit card and the charge slip. He scribbled his signature without checking the amount. Whatever she had charged him, it was worth every penny. As she handed him the receipt, his cell phone rang.

"Mulder," he said into the phone.

He heard sobbing on the other end. A girl was crying, trying to speak, but he couldn't make out the words.

"What?" Mulder said. "Please, I can't—"

"I know who the killer is," the girl on the other end of the line said. "I know who did it all." The girl started crying again.

"Who is this?" Mulder asked, trying to project professional caring across the invisible connection.

The sobbing continued, until finally the girl broke off long enough to manage, "This is Margi Kleinjan."

"Margi," said Mulder, remembering the name. She was one of the girls they had interviewed, one of the girls who claimed they had seen the evil cult at work. "Where are you, Margi?" he asked. "Just tell me where you are . . ."

Scully and Detective White braced themselves for a confrontation as the bobbing flashlights drew closer down the bird-spattered road. The two stepped into the path of the onrushing posse in an attempt to intercept them. These people didn't look like they were fooling around.

Especially Bob Spitz, who, carrying his hunting rifle, led the group.

"I don't know where you think you're going," Scully said to him as the group came to a restless halt in front of her. "But I suggest you put that gun down, sir, or I'm going to have to arrest you."

"We're not standing around anymore," Spitz shouted at Scully. "We're gonna take care of this ourselves!"

Scully tried to reason with him. "But you can't go walking down the middle of the street carrying a loaded weapon. It's against the law."

Bob Spitz winked at her and spoke in a surprisingly reasonable voice. "Not if I'm hunting, it's not." Then his voice broke, and he raised the weapon to the sky, almost howling, "Are we ready to hunt?"

The people behind him roared their approval.

Scully spoke to Bob Spitz with every ounce of reason she was able to muster, emphasizing each individual word. "There's no one to hunt. There are no satanists here."

"Then who killed those kids?" Bob Spitz demanded. He glanced at the road and added, "And who killed all these birds?"

A shrill cry interrupted them. "Help me! Somebody, help!"

Terri Roberts came running into the circle

illuminated by the flashlights.

"I know who the killer is," she said.

Everyone stood in shocked silence. Even Bob Spitz was speechless.

Terri looked from face to face. Her own face was streaked with tears, but her voice was calm. "I know who did it all . . ."

Mulder stepped into Scott Simmons's garage. The first thing he saw was the boy's body. Heat was still escaping through the hole in Scott's back in a thin trail of steam. And sitting on the floor beside him was Margi, crying desperately. Mulder helped her up.

"Margi, come on. Let's get you out of here."

"She killed him," Margi whimpered.

"Who?"

"Terri. She killed all of them."

"Terri Roberts? She killed all the high-school boys?"

"And Brenda Summerfield, too," Margi added.

"How did she do it? . . ."

". . . How did she do it?" asked Scully.

"I think Margi's been possessed by the devil," cried Terri Roberts. She stood before Scully, Detective White, and the crowd of angry townsfolk. "She . . . she killed Scott Simmons tonight, with a garage-door spring. I don't know how she does it. I think she's evil . . ."

". . . I think she's evil," Margi told Mulder. Without even knowing it, she was mimicking Terri's every word, every movement. "She tricked Boom into going up on that cliff— then she hanged him, and laughed about it, just like she laughed about Eric Bauer in the gym last night. She made all the lights go out, and he was trapped under the bleachers. She could hear him screaming, but she wouldn't stop!"

"Why didn't *you* stop her, Margi? Why didn't you tell anyone?"

Margi's eyes darted back and forth, as if she just realized it had been a possibility.

"Because I was afraid. And because we're best friends. And best friends are supposed to stick by each other." And then she broke down in tears, unable to say anything more.

Scully comforted the crying Terri, finally able to feel something for this girl now that she was no longer telling fables about cults.

Margi Kleinjan, thought Scully. She should have realized it.

Chapter Sixteen

Over the wind and Terri's sobs, Scully heard the faint chirping of the cell phone in her coat pocket. It must be Mulder checking in. Whatever happened to him?

She pulled out the phone and flipped it open, heading away from Terri and the angry mob toward her car, where she would be able to hear clearly and speak freely.

"Yes?"

"Scully, it's me."

"Where are you?" Scully asked into the phone, shutting the car door behind her. Through the windshield she kept an eye on the crowd outside.

"I'm at a crime scene," Mulder said. "A new one. I think I've finally got a solid lead in these deaths."

Scully let her lips curl into a satisfied smile.

"I'm way ahead of you, Mulder," she said, trying not to let the glee seep into her voice. "There's a suspect I want to bring in."

"Who's that?" he asked quickly.

"Margi Kleinjan," said Scully triumphantly.

Across town in Scott Simmons's garage, Mulder glanced over at Margi Kleinjan standing next to Scott's pickup. Mulder moved farther away from her and spoke as softly as he could into the phone. "Margi Kleinjan?" he asked.

"That's right," Scully said. "Her friend just gave us a statement."

Mulder shook his head, feeling sorry for his partner. "Actually, I'm way ahead of *you*, Scully. I'm standing here with Margi Kleinjan right now." He couldn't quite keep the smirk out of his voice. "Only she just gave me a statement implicating *her* friend."

"Who?" Scully's voice demanded.

Uh-oh, thought Mulder. That "Who?" of hers didn't sound appropriately humble. In fact, it sounded like she was anticipating what he was going to say next.

"Terri Roberts," Mulder said, less decisively than he would have liked.

Scully looked out the windshield of the rental car at Terri, who was talking with Detective White.

"Well, actually I'm even *further* ahead of *you*, Mulder," Scully snapped into her phone, "because I'm here with Terri right now."

"You are?"

Scully sighed. "Look, Mulder," she said wearily, "I've got your suspect, and you've got mine. Why does that make sense to me at this point?"

They had been at each other's throats since they started this case, Scully realized. She didn't know why, and she didn't like it. And now each of their key witnesses was the other's prime suspect. This was a bad situation. Very bad.

Across town, Mulder rubbed his temples with one hand while still holding the phone in the other. He had to think. It wasn't easy, and that was unusual. What had Zirinka said? Something about forces. Something that he had a feeling would explain what was happening right now between him and Scully.

Then he remembered.

"Relationships are going to suffer," Zirinka had said.

"Scully," Mulder said into the phone. He was serious now. No more attitude, no more weariness. He had to get through to her. He had to be clear. He knew that their perceptions were clouded, that each was hearing things the other hadn't intended, and saying things they didn't mean.

Relationships are going to suffer.

Why hadn't Zirinka been more specific? Mulder thought savagely. He suddenly knew what she *really* meant: Relationships are going to *end.*

"Listen to me, Scully," he said. "I think I know what's going on here."

He knew, as soon as the words came out of mouth, that it was the wrong thing to say. She would take it the wrong way. He could practically feel her rolling her eyes on the other end of the phone. He had to reach her somehow. He had to say something that would get through to her.

"You were right all along, Scully," he said desperately. "You were right—this has nothing to do with cults."

He paused. He heard nothing on the other end of the line.

"Meet me at the police station. We'll get formal statements. I think we can sort this whole thing out."

He waited. Still no response. Had he gotten through to her? Or had she heard his pleading as patronizing? Had she already hung up?

"Scully?" he gasped into the phone.

"Sure." Scully's voice sounded very far away . . . distant . . . cold. "Fine. Whatever."

Chapter Seventeen

In the clear night sky Uranus hung five degrees directly above Mars, and a hundred degrees directly above Mercury. At midnight, the three planets would be in perfect alignment.

It was 11:57 P.M.

Mulder arrived at the police station first with Margi in tow, her teased hair wild with static electricity, her layer of overdone makeup smudged across her face like a ruined oil painting. With his arm firmly gripping her cheerleader jacket, Mulder quickly steered her past the receptionist and into the squad room, where half a dozen exhausted cops were tending to Comity's worst night in history.

Mulder sat Margi down beside an empty desk. The girl seemed distraught, even vulnerable. But for once Mulder felt no sympathy—

only a desire to end this, any way possible.

"Detective White's cat?" Mulder asked.

Margi nodded sadly. "Terri did that, too. It was horrible."

They were interrupted by the sound of screeching tires outside. Mulder knew that Scully and Detective White had arrived with the other girl. Mulder couldn't help wondering what would happen when they were brought together—

But it began even before Terri arrived in the room. It started with the look on Margi's face. As the footsteps of her former best friend drew nearer, Margi's distressed expression suddenly turned stone cold, as if Terri's very presence altered her in some way.

There were several small TVs gracing the officers' desks. Suddenly they all switched on—and although they were set to different channels, they all played the same old silent movie. *The Keystone Kops*. Even the video surveillance screen displayed the pie-fighting, trigger-happy, sorry excuses for law enforcement.

And then things began to move.

At first it seemed like a small tremor. Pencils and coffee mugs began to jitter on the desks. But in a moment the desks themselves began to vibrate. Small objects flew in all directions. Filing cabinets slid open, dumping their contents onto the floor. And then, in a single motion, everything—*everything*—from the solid-oak desks to the two-ton safe, began to shimmy across the floor, turning and colliding like bumper cars as they picked up speed. Officers dove for cover, to escape the skittering furniture.

CRASH: As if drawn by incredibly strong magnets, all of the furniture suddenly pushed away from the center of the room and smashed against the four walls.

Terri Roberts walked through the door.

Now, with everything pushed away, the room looked like an arena: an oval of scuffed tile into which Terri Roberts and Margi Kleinjan stepped like two prizefighters.

"Hey, girlfriend," spat one, with lethal venom in her voice.

"Hey, girlfriend," echoed the other, in a black, malignant tone.

The walls, which had never stopped shaking, began to reverberate more violently as the girls stared at each other across the chasm between them.

"Get her out of here," Mulder shouted to Scully.

BAM! He was answered by the blast of a gun. Someone had fired a weapon! Suddenly he realized that it was *his* gun—although it was still holstered. It had blown a hole straight through his jacket!

BAM! BAM! Suddenly gunfire began to erupt all around them. The officers' revolvers fired randomly, blowing holes in the walls. Bullets ricocheted around the room like angry hornets. Everyone but the two girls ducked for cover as a rack of shotguns on the wall exploded.

POP! The fuses blew next, and the entire building was plunged into darkness. Coughing in the acrid smoke of burned gunpowder, Mulder scrambled out from behind a desk. He tried to make his way across the debris, smashing his shins and tumbling over the barricade of furniture between him and the girls. Finally he reached Margi Kleinjan. He grabbed her and dragged her to the nearest door. Kicking it open, he yanked her into a hallway, the glass from broken lightbulbs crunching beneath his feet in the darkness. He could see the static crackling in Margi's hair and, in her eyes, the look of clouds before a killer storm.

There was a door at the end of the hall. The storage closet. He dragged the struggling teen to the door, pulled it open, and forced her inside. He slammed the door shut and leaned against it, barricading her in.

But still the walls in the hallway shook all around him.

Terri Roberts thundered down the hall toward him, with Scully trying to catch up behind her.

"Out of my way," Terri hissed at Mulder, with something beyond murder in her eyes.

Mulder felt those eyes burning through him, and he had to step aside. Terri threw the door open and entered the room for the final confrontation with her unnatural twin.

"What is going on here?" asked Scully as Mulder slammed the heavy door.

"Do you really want to know?" Mulder answered.

Scully hesitated; perhaps she didn't.

Around them the walls shuddered more violently every moment, and the linoleum tiles began to buckle as though the floor were a snake about to shed.

Mulder's eyes shot to the clock on the wall. Then he looked at his watch.

It was thirty seconds to midnight.

Around them the emergency lights suddenly flickered and buzzed until their halogen lamps blew out. Tiles peeled up from the floor and fell from the ceiling. Glass picture frames exploded on the walls.

Mulder looked at the clock again in the cataclysm. It was five seconds to midnight.

The rattling around them grew deafening.

Four seconds.

The cinder-block walls began to grind themselves into dust.

Three seconds.

The hinges of the door melted. The knob shot from the jamb like a cork from a bottle.

Two.

The pipes above them imploded.

One.

Mulder felt the pressure of everything he had experienced over the last two days tear at the seams of his skull. This had to end. *This had to end—NOW!*

Midnight.

CRASH! Every window in the building shattered, and the sound echoed into the distance. Then Mulder realized that it wasn't an echo—it was the sound of every window, every piece of glass in the town of Comity, detonating as the shock wave surged out from this very point in space, from this very point in time.

And then silence.

What had taken weeks to build was over in an instant. The power of the planetary alignment crescendoed and faded the instant it peaked.

Mulder looked at Scully in the settling

dust, and she held his gaze. The coldness was gone from her eyes.

Relief flooded through him. The cosmic event was over. The planets had passed their syzygy and were now diverging at hundreds of miles per minute. It was all over.

Just then, they heard angry voices down the hall. Bob Spitz and his mob were spilling toward them. As usual, Spitz had his shotgun at the ready.

"Put that gun down!" Mulder and Scully yelled simultaneously.

"Where are they?" Spitz screamed. "The girls!"

Mulder gestured toward the closed door behind him. "In there," he said.

Spitz moved forward. "I think we'll just see for ourselves."

The crowd, no longer knowing how to feel, focused all of their attention on the closet door. Practically wrenched loose, it hung precariously from its hinges. Bob Spitz was the first person to move toward the opening.

Mulder gently put a hand to his chest to stop

him. "I don't think you want to go in there."

But the look in Spitz's eyes made it very clear that he did. It wasn't the look of a wild man anymore, but of a man who needed to know what he had just lived through.

And so Mulder opened the door. The stone walls now glowed red-hot like the walls of a furnace. Or of hell.

"It won't be a pretty sight," said Scully, and Mulder nodded in agreement. But as they stepped into the room, where the floor was so hot it began to melt the soles of their shoes, they heard soft, helpless weeping.

There, in the corner, huddled the two girls, lost and uncomprehending, more frightened and horrified than any of them. Innocents once again.

Bob Spitz, his eyes suddenly seeming much older, looked at the girls, and the walls, and the people around him, then finally down to his own hands, which still held the shotgun.

"My God," he mumbled, closing his weary eyes. "I think it *was* Satan."

Chapter Eighteen

Scully and Mulder returned to their motel and picked up their bags. They could have left in the morning, but neither had any desire to spend one more night in Comity.

While Mulder threw the bags into the trunk, Scully got into the driver's seat and started the car. Mulder took the passenger side, offering no resistance.

As they drove from the town, Mulder gazed up at the pinpoints of light in the sky.

The universe was truly unfathomable—something people took for granted.

There is so much we think we know, thought Mulder. *And so often, we refuse to believe that the grand and noble forces of the universe could have any more effect on us than a butterfly beating its wings halfway around the world.*

Scully silently increased their speed as they pulled onto the familiar main road that would lead them out of town. And Mulder let his mind drift back to the girls.

Was it really so strange that two girls born on the same date, at the same time, in the same place, would find themselves the unfortunate focus of unseen forces? That they could have the power to converge like the planets themselves into burning pinpoints of cosmic energy, whose absolute gravity would threaten to swallow and consume everything in its path?

Mulder peered out his window, just in time to catch the flash of a red sign flying by.

"Uh, Scully . . . wasn't that a stop sign you just ran?"

"Oh, shut up, Mulder," Scully said. But she gave him a wry smile.

Mulder just grinned and shrugged it off. "Sure. Fine. Whatever."

The End

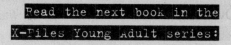
Read the next book in the
X-Files Young Adult series:

The X-Files #4: **OUR TOWN**
by Eric Elfman

from Chapter One

Taking a deep breath, George opened his door and tumbled out of the car. He looked in the direction that Paula had disappeared, but all he could see was a thick tangle of trees.

"Paula!" he called. "Paula! Where are you?"

"Over here, George! Come on!"

George could hear her voice coming from deep within the woods. He unhappily realized what he had to do now. Scowling, George started toward the trees.

"All right, Paula!" he called out again. "I'm coming! Which way?"

"Over here, George! Hurry!"

Her voice floated to him through the forest, and he followed it, starting to trot.

Overweight and far from fit, he was soon sweating from the exertion. His heavy puffs of breath condensed in the damp night air, becoming a vapor trail that hung behind him.

"Come on, George . . ." He could hear Paula's tinkling laughter just up ahead.

George struggled up a low hill, through some brambles and low bushes. The darkness inside the woods was nearly complete. As he moved toward her voice, he kept his hands out in front of him, swatting at branches as he stumbled along.

"Paula," he cried plaintively, as he entered a small clearing. "Where are you? I'm too old for these kinds of—*oof!*" He had meant to say "games" as he tripped over a thick root and nose-dived into the hard ground.

George stayed down for a moment, gasping for breath. Slowly, shakily, he got to his knees.

A few inches away he saw a swarm of fireflies. He blinked his eyes and refocused. No, they weren't inches away—they were all the way across the clearing.

And they weren't fireflies.

They were balls of bouncing light. Dozens of them.

Coming his way.

George rose unsteadily to his feet. He didn't know what they were, and didn't want to know. He didn't know where Paula was, either, and at this point he didn't care. All he wanted to do was to get out of these woods.

He turned as he heard a rustling behind him.

"Paula? Paula, is that you?"

Suddenly the branches parted, and an enormous face stared back at him, inches from his own.

But it wasn't a human face—it was some sort of grotesque mask. The head was surrounded by a blur of fiery red. Angry streaks of yellow were splayed across its cheeks. The hideous thing's eyes and mouth were outlined in a white so bright, they shone even in the dark.

George, too frightened to make a sound, took an involuntary step back.

Then he saw the ax.

The monster lifted the weapon high over George's head, and George finally managed to let out a scream. Then they were both screaming as the creature plunged the ax down toward George's throat.

Only George's scream stopped when the ax drove home, as all the lights went out and his world was plunged into yet another kind of darkness . . .